VAN BUREN PUBLIC LIBRARY

```
   1/92        J/796.9
                Sports set

  Italia, Bob

  Snowboarding
```

2. A fine will be charged on each book which is not returned according to the above rule. No book will be issued to any person incurring such a fine until it has been paid.

3. All injuries to books beyond reasonable wear and all losses shall be made good to the satisfaction of the Librarian.

4. Each borrower is held responsible for all books drawn on his card and for all fines accruing on the same.

Action Sports Library

Snowboarding

Bob Italia

Published by Abdo & Daughters, 6535 Cecilia Circle, Edina, Minnesota 55439.

Library bound edition distributed by Rockbottom Books, Pentagon Tower, P.O. Box 36036, Minneapolis, Minnesota 55435.

Copyright© 1991 by Abdo Consulting Group, Inc., Pentagon Tower, P.O. Box 36036, Minneapolis, Minnesota 55435. International copyrights reserved in all countries. No part of this book may be reproduced in any form without written permission from the publisher.

Printed in the United States.

ISBN: 1-56239-073-2

Library of Congress Card Catalog Number: 91-073024

Cover Photos: ©ALLSPORT USA/PHOTOGRAPHER, 1991.
Inside Photos: ©ALLSPORT USA/PHOTOGRAPHER, 1991.

Warning: The series *Action Sports Library* is intended as entertainment for children. These sporting activities should never be attempted without the proper conditioning, training, instruction, supervision, and equipment.

Edited by Rosemary Wallner

CONTENTS

It All Started in the Mid-1960s 5

Snowboard Design 6

What to Wear..................................8

Practice, Practice, Practice 10

Are You "Goofy-Footed?"................11

Getting Up the Slope 12

How Do You Steer this Thing? 14

How To Fall 16

Snowboarding Rule 17

How to Become a Certified Snowboarder 19

Freestyle Snowboarding 21

The Halfpipe......................................23

The Backscratcher 25

Competition Snowboarding..............26

A Final Word......................................29

Glossary 30

Snowboarding—the hottest sport on snow!

SNOWBOARDING

It All Started in the Mid-1960s

New Jersey teenager Tom Sims was frustrated. He loved to go skateboarding. But during the winter, the streets near his home were usually covered with ice or snow. How could he possibly use his skateboard?

Then Sims got an idea. He went to his junior high woodshop classroom and, using a skateboard design, came up with a skateboard for ice and snow.

His first design did not work well. But in 1969, Sims finally perfected his winter skateboard idea. Snowboarding was born!

Snowboarding did not catch on quickly with the public. People thought they could control the snowboards. Insurance companies would not give policies to the manufacturers of these boards. And ski resort owners wouldn't allow them on the slopes for fear of being sued if an accident occurred. Besides, snowboarding seemed to be a fad, not a real sport.

Gradually, snowboarding began to catch on with the public. Snowboarding was featured in the James Bond movie *A View to a Kill*. It has been used in television commercials. An international competition called the World Cup was formed. And a certification program was established to set safety guidelines and techniques. Today, over 250,000 people enjoy snowboarding.

Snowboard Design

Today's snowboard is much different than Sims' original plywood and rope design. It is made of laminated wood with a foam core. Steel edges make "carving" (turning) easier. Today's snowboard is much faster and more

Snowboarding • 7

Wearing the proper clothing will make
snowboarding more fun.

controllable than the early design. A typical snowboard costs $150 or more.

You don't need special boots or poles to snowboard. All that's needed are bindings and a leash. The bindings hold your feet to the board. The leash, a nylon strap, is attached to the board and prevents it from getting away from you should you happen to fall. The leash is fastened around the leg and secured with a plastic buckle.

Regular snow boots are recommended for snowboarding. If you have the extra money, you can get specially-designed snowboard boots. The soft boot costs between $50 and $150. The hard boot, which looks like a typical ski boot, costs between $100 and $300.

What to Wear

Many snowboarders wear blue jeans. But blue jeans can get wet and make your journey down the hill or mountain very uncomfort-

Snowboarding • 9

To perform stunts, you need lots of practice.

able—and cold! Insulated ski pants will keep you warm and dry. A lightweight insulated jacket is also recommended.

Ski gloves do an excellent job of keeping your hands warm. But there are specially designed snowboarding gloves. They have longer cuffs that fit tightly over your sleeve. And they have extra padding across the back. Goggles are also recommended. They protect your eyes from the sun, wind and glare.

Practice, Practice, Practice

Mastering the snowboard isn't as easy as it looks. Like any sport activity, it takes a lot of time and practice to become a good snowboarder.

Before you go out and buy a snowboard, rent one first (the rental fee is usually $15 a day). That way, you'll find out if you even like the sport before you spend a lot of money on it. Most ski resorts rent snowboards. Don't rent a board that's too big (adult versions are 62 and 70 inches long). There are smaller boards for younger riders (56 and 51 inches long). They're a lot easier to control. Make sure you're wearing the boots you'll be using for snowboarding.

Once you have your snowboard, you will want to take a lesson. Don't expect to step onto the board and glide gracefully down the hill. You have to learn how to stop and turn on the board first. Skipping the beginner's lesson will only increase the risk of harm to yourself—and others.

Are You "Goofy-Footed?"

Most snowboarders ride with the left foot forward. A "goofy-footed" snowboarder rides with the right foot forward. There is no right or wrong way. Choose the method that is most comfortable for you.

Getting Up the Slope

Once you've determined the proper stance, you'll have to get yourself to the chair lift. Unfasten the back boot and use this foot to propel you to the lift. Once it's your turn to get on a chair, make sure the snowboard is facing forward. Then as the chair reaches you, sit down and grab the side or back. The chair will lift you and the board comfortably off the ground.

As you're climbing the hill, you may notice that the snowboard is dangling wildly. To prevent this, rest the board on the top of your free foot. Once you reach the top, point the snowboard upward. When the snowboard meets the snow, stand and place your free foot in front of the rear binding. Then let the chair push you along the exit slope. Glide to a safe spot before you stop to secure the back boot. There will be other people behind you coming off the exit slope. If you stop too soon, you may create a hazard.

Snowboarding • 13

Carving the slope on a snowboard.

How Do You Steer this Thing?

Before you head down the slope, you need to assume the proper stance. Bend your knees slightly, place your weight on the front foot, and keep your arms outstretched for balance. Then practice the side-slip maneuver. This controls speed and allows you to stop.

To perform the side-slip, place the edge of the snowboard across the slope and face your body uphill. As you dig the sides of the board into the snow, the board will slow. The more pressure you use, the slower you will slide. If you want to stop but the board keeps slipping, just sit down. Then try again. With a little practice, you'll learn how to control the board—instead of it controlling you!

Next you'll want to practice turning the snowboard. The snowboard will travel in the direction it's pointed. To point the board where *you* want it to go, use the *hand* that is over the front foot. If you want to go left, point your hand to the left. If you want to go right, point your hand to the right.

Everytime you turn, you'll also need to pivot your back foot. But remember, keep your weight on the front foot. This allows you to move the back foot more easily.

Now practice your turning. Keep your weight on the front foot. Point left with your hand. Pivot the back foot. Point, pivot. Point, pivot. The more you practice, the smoother and easier it becomes.

A version of the side-slip is the *forward* side-slip. In this maneuver, your body faces downhill instead of uphill. Dig the edge of the board into the snow with your heels. Point and pivot to turn. Each version of the side-slip is designed to get you down a hill that is too steep to head straight down.

How To Fall

Nobody likes to fall then they're skiing or snowboarding. It's embarrassing, and you could get hurt. But knowing how to fall can make the difference between a bruised ego and a broken wrist.

The most common snowboard injury is to the wrist and upper body. A snowboarder will try to break the fall by landing on his hands. This puts too much pressure on the wrists and may cause a fracture. If you find yourself falling forward, land on your forearms. If you are falling backwards, land on your rear. Once you see that the way is clear, pick yourself up, dust yourself off, and try again. The more you practice, the better you will become.

Snowboarding Rules

One of the problems snowboarding had during the early years was a view that snowboarders were wild and out-of-control. Everything you do on your snowboard will influence public opinion of the sport. To keep the slopes safe—and to keep snowboards on the slopes—follow these basic rules:

- Always be in control of your snowboard. Don't make quick turns without looking.

- When you're about to pass someone, make sure they hear you coming. Call out, "On your left" or "On your right."

- Never cut in front of someone.

- Don't stop in a narrow slope. If you fall, move to the side as quickly as possible. This includes falling on the exit slope of the chair lift.

- Always allow skiers the right-of-way.

18 • *Action Sports Library*

Catching air!

Snowboarding can be fun and exciting. If you can show others that snowboarders are courteous and responsible, ski resorts will gladly welcome you.

How to Become a Certified Snowboarder

Though many ski resorts recognize snowboarding as a legitimate sport, some resorts refuse to let snowboarders on the slopes unless they have a certification card. To get one, you'll need to take a certification class. They are offered at most ski resorts.

In certification class, you will learn all the snowboarding techniques and rules described in this book. When you show the instructor that you know the rules and can snowboard responsibly and with control, you will be awarded your certification.

Performing a handstand on the halfpipe.

Freestyle Snowboarding

Once you've mastered the boarding techniques, you may want to consider freestyle snowboarding. It's not for everybody. Freestyle snowboarding involves "catching air"—aerials!

If you're a beginner, select a small drop off of two or three feet. As you make your approach, keep your knees bent. If you feel tense or are traveling too fast, don't attempt the jump. Only make the attempt if you feel comfortable.

When you reach the drop off, spring off the top by extending your legs. Make sure your arms are extended about waist high for the proper balance. And keep the tip of the board up. When you're in the air, bring your legs back to your body. By the time you hit the peak of your airborne jump, your legs should be completely pulled up.

The backscratcher.

As you make your descent, keep the tip of the board up and carefully extend your legs again. When the board hits the snow, cushion the landing by flexing your legs.

The Halfpipe

Halfpipes—narrow snow trenches with curved walls—are becoming a common sight on the slopes. They are specifically designed for freestyle snowboarding. With more and more snowboarders using them, it's important to know some basic rules:

- Always wait your turn.

- Always wait until the snowboarder in front of you is completely through the halfpipe before you start your run.

- Start your run by calling out, "Dropping!" This alerts others that you are entering the halfpipe.

24 • *Action Sports Library*

Competition snowboarding.
Notice the protective gear!

- When you reach the end, exit the halfpipe immediately. Don't wait around and watch. You may create a hazard.

- Never stand on the rim of the halfpipe to watch your fellow freestylers. They may glide up the side of the pipe and accidentally strike you.

The Backscratcher

The "backscratcher" is another form of freestyle snowboarding. Once you are airborne, bend your legs up behind you so that the snowboard touches your back. It's important that you get enough height on your jump, or you won't have time to bring the board back down for a safe landing.

If you really want to spice up your airborne jumps, try a mid-air turn like the "backside air." Find a halfpipe, then glide up one side. Once you are at the peak of your airborne stunt, turn your snowboard 180 degrees and come back down into the halfpipe.

Whether you perform airborne stunts, or just traverse the slope, never attempt any maneuver unless you're comfortable. Talk to experienced freestyle snowboarders and find out all you can about the airborne stunts before you attempt your first jump.

Competition Snowboarding

Once you've become an accomplished freestyle snowboarder, you may want to consider testing your skills and your nerve against other snowboarders. Many ski resorts organize freestyle and slalom competitions.

The United States Amateur Snowboard Association sponsors many events across the country. There's even a Juniors division for young people 17 years old and younger.

For the really serious competitor, there's the World Cup, sponsored by the North American Snowboard Association (NASBA) and the Snowboarding European Association (SEA).

The World Cup is a series of four international races. It has two divisions: Men's and Women's. The winner of each division is considered the world snowboarding champion.

The World Cup events test four different snowboarding abilities: slalom (zigzagging around obstacles), downhill, halfpipe, and moguls (large mounds of snow). Anyone who wants to be considered for the overall championship must compete in at least three of the World Cup events. The snowboarder with the most points wins the title.

Champion snowboarders can make good money. A common first prize is $25,000. More and more corporations are sponsoring snowboard competitions. The prize money is certain to increase. There's even talk about making snowboarding an Olympic event. But first it has to be approved as an Olympic exhibition sport.

To learn more about how to compete in snowboarding events, write to the snowboard organization in your area. Here are the addresses of a few organizations:

- Canadian Snowboard Association
  609 Denman Street
  Vancouver, B.C. V6-2L3

- North American Snowboard Association
  P.O. Box 38836
  Denver, CO 80238

- United States Amateur Snowboard Association
  P.O. Box 251
  Green Valley Lake, CA 92341

There are also some snowboarding publications that keep tabs on the latest equipment, snowboarding techniques, and competition. Here are the most popular ones:

- *Snowboarder*
  P.O. Box 1028
  Dana Point, CA 92629

- *International Snowboard Magazine*
  P.O. Box 170309
  San Francisco, CA 94117

- *Transworld Snowboarding Magazine*
  P.O. Box 6
  Cardiff, CA 92007

A Final Word

Snowboarding can be an exciting and challenging sport. To make it safe and respectable, always exercise caution and courtesy. You'll get more enjoyment out of it, and earn the admiration of skiers and fellow snowboarders everywhere.

GLOSSARY

- Aerials—snowboarding stunts that use jumps.

- Backscratcher—a type of freestyle stunt where the snowboard touches your back.

- Backside air—a type of freestyle stunt where you turn 180 degrees in the air.

- Binding—the mechanism that holds your boot to the snowboard.

- Carving—making sharp turns inthe snow.

- Forward side-slip—a maneuver that allows you to snowboard across a slope facing downhill.

- Freestyle—a type of snowboarding style that uses stunts.

- Goofy-footed—a snowboarder who rides with his right foot forward.

- Halfpipe—narrow snow trenches with curved walls.

- Leash—the nylon strap that keeps the snowboard from running away from you in the event of a fall.

- Moguls—large mounds of snow.

- Pivot—turning the board aroundquickly in one motion.

- Side-slip—a maneuver that allows you to snowboard across a slope with your back facing downhill.

- Slalom—a zigzagging snowboard race course.

VAN BUREN PUBLIC LIBRARY